Hanukkah Lights

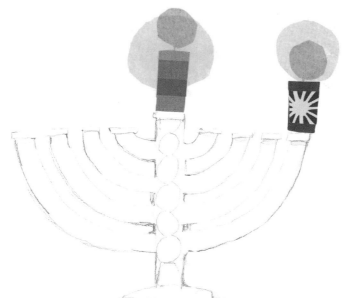

David Martin   illustrated by Melissa Sweet

CANDLEWICK PRESS

It's Hanukkah!

This is our menorah
with candles ready to light.

Hanukkah candles,
shining bright.

One more candle
every night.

Latkes tonight.
Mmm–mmm . . . good.

Tonight let's play dreidel.
Spin, spin, spin, little top!

Tonight we give presents.

Thank you.
Thank you.

Hanukkah gelt
is our treat tonight.

Shiny gold,
then yummy sweet!

Let's make shadows
in the light.

Sing and dance,
sing and dance.
Now's our chance
to sing and dance.

Time for a story.

My big sister can read to me.

Tonight it's a feast!

At last, every candle in,
every candle glowing.

Menorah candles
burning bright

Say happy Hanukkah
every night.

First paperback sticker edition 2015

Library of Congress Catalog Card Number 2009920350
ISBN 978-0-7636-3029-4 (board book)
ISBN 978-0-7636-7972-9 (paperback with stickers)

15 16 17 18 19 20 APS 10 9 8 7 6 5 4 3 2 1

Printed in Humen, Dongguan, China

This book was typeset in Avril.
The illustrations were done in watercolor and collage.

Candlewick Press
99 Dover Street
Somerville, Massachusetts 02144

visit us at www.candlewick.com